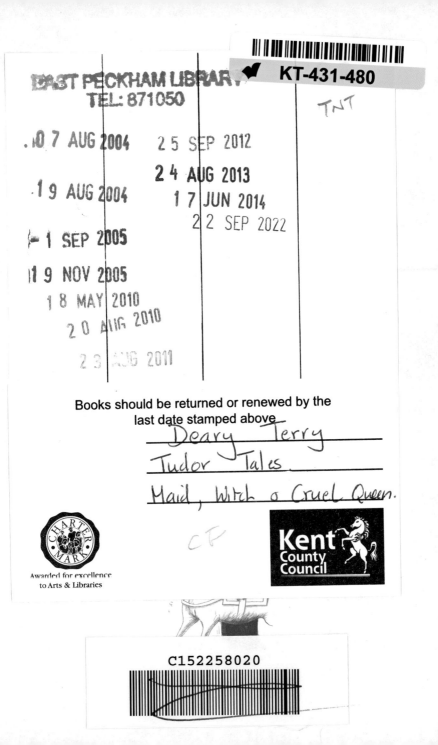

Books should be returned or renewed by the
last date stamped above

Deary   Terry

Tudor   Tales.

Maid, Witch & Cruel Queen.

CF

*This book is dedicated to the memory
of the tens of thousands of harmless men,
women and children who suffered horribly because
of silly superstitions about witchcraft – Terry Deary*

First published 2003 by
A & C Black Publishers Ltd
37 Soho Square, London W1D 3QZ
www.acblack.com

Text copyright © 2003 Terry Deary
Illustrations copyright © 2003 Helen Flook

The rights of Terry Deary and Helen Flook to be identified
as the author and illustrator of this work respectively have been
asserted by them in accordance with the Copyrights, Designs
and Patents Act 1988.

ISBN 0-7136-6432-0

A CIP catalogue for this book is available from the
British Library.

A & C Black uses paper produced with elemental
chlorine-free pulp, harvested from managed sustainable forests.

Printed and bound in Spain by G. Z. Printek, Bilbao.

1 The messenger in red and gold

I remember the day Queen Mary Tudor came to our town. It was the most fearsome, exciting and heart-stopping day of my life. I'll remember it if I live to be a hundred.

I was a serving girl at Lord Scuggate's manor house – a small castle, really. And I was invisible!

No, really! I carried the food and the wine from the kitchen to the table and all the grand folk in the great hall ignored me.

They never said 'Please', they just held out a wine cup to be filled. They never, ever said 'Thanks!' It was as if I wasn't there. Invisible in my shabby black dress.

My mouth stayed shut. But my eyes could
see and my ears could hear. That summer
evening there was a sudden hammering on
the door. Lord Scuggate looked furious.

'Who dares to knock at a Scuggate door
that way?' he demanded.

I hurried over the rushes on the stone
floor and opened the door. A young man
in a coat of blood red and gold threw
his handsome head up and
marched in. The hounds
by the fireside
growled.

'Lord Scuggate of Bewcastle?' the young man asked and his voice whined like a leaking trumpet.

'Who wants to know?' his Lordship
asked. 'What sort of slabberdegullion are
you to come barging in on Lord Scuggate
and his guests?'

Sir James Marley of Roughsike squeaked
and tried to shake Lord
Scuggate's arm.

His Lordship shook him off.

'I'll have you stripped and whipped and dragged at the cart's tail all the way to the gallows!' he yelled at the messenger.

He swelled like a pig's bladder that the boys blow up to play football. His face was purple.

'I'll have you ...'

'No, your Lordship!' Sir James squawked. 'Look at the badge on his coat.'

'Shut up, man,' Lord Scuggate snapped without taking his eyes off the messenger. 'I'll have you hanged by the neck and I don't care who your master is ...'

'Mistress,' the shocked messenger mumbled.

'Who your mistress is!' Lord Scuggate snorted. 'I see by your badge you wear the sign of ...'

He stopped. Everyone was looking at the floor. Even the dogs that chewed their bones stopped their crunching.

The only sound was Lord Scuggate spluttering as if someone had stuck a needle in his pig-bladder face. '... the sign of ... er ... the sign of ...'

'Her Majesty Queen Mary Tudor of England,' the messenger said quietly.

Lord Scuggate grinned weakly showing his broken and yellow teeth. 'And you are very, very welcome to Bewcastle Hall, my dear young friend!'

2 The cruel killing Queen

The messenger had said that the Queen would be passing through Bewcastle on a tour of the Scottish Borders. She would stop at Scuggate Hall for lunch the next day.

When the young man in red and gold had gone, the Bewcastle men muttered over their wine cups as the invisible maid heard their terrible talk.

'Down in London they call the Queen "Bloody Mary" because she burns anyone who doesn't worship at a Catholic church,' Sir James Marley of Roughsike said quietly.

'She'd burn us if she found anyone who doesn't go to church,' Father Walton of Catlowdy Church warned them.

Lord Scuggate looked at him sharply. 'It's your job to make sure people go to church,' he said.

The priest in the velvet cloak spread his hands and smirked. 'My Lord, it is you the Queen will blame and you the Queen will burn.'

Lord Scuggate's blotched face turned pale. 'Everyone in Bewcastle goes to church … well … they go Easter and Christmas anyway, don't they?'

The men brought their heads closer together.

'We could get all the Bewcastle folk together and have a march through the town to the church, just as Queen Mary arrives,' Father Walton said.

'All carrying crosses,' Sir James Marley added.

'And singing hymns,' Lord Scuggate put in. 'The Queen will love that!'

'Would the town people do it?' Father Walton asked, and his bald head shone yellow in the light of the torches.

'They will if we promise them a few barrels of beer!' Lord Scuggate chuckled.

The men laughed and held out their wine cups for me to fill.

'Old Nan doesn't drink,' Father Walton said.

Lord Scuggate sighed.

'Who's Old Nan?' Sir James asked as he cleaned his fingernails with his knife.

'A wise woman who lives out at Butterburn in the hills,' Lord Scuggate snapped. 'Some say she is a witch. But the truth is she just mixes herbs and cures made from the plants on the moors. I use them myself,' he said. 'But you wouldn't get her into a church or singing hymns.'

'Perfect!' Sir James cried and waved his knife. 'Queen Mary likes to see her sort burned.'

'So?' Lord Scuggate growled.

'So … burn her! Tomorrow at noon in the market square. Queen Mary will thank you for the rest of her blood-soaked life!'

'Perfect!' Lord Scuggate chuckled. 'Tomorrow at dawn we find Old Nan.'

'She could be out on the moors, collecting herbs at this time of the year,' the priest reminded him.

'We'll track her down. That's what my hunting dogs are for,' he said, and threw a scrap of meat to the snapping hounds on the floor.

Lord Scuggate raised his wine cup and clashed it against the raised cups of the other two.

'Here's to good Queen Mary ... and a death to all her enemies – especially Old Nan!'

I cleared the tables after their lordships
had staggered to their beds. Then I crept
back down to the main hall and found the
two shaggy hounds asleep by the guttering
fire. I fed them with plates of meat till they
could eat no more.

They groaned,
rolled over and slept.

But I couldn't sleep. I had work to do.

I took a black woollen cloak from the stables and slipped out into the cool light of the quarter moon. Rats scuttered out of my way as I padded across the yard in my bare feet and on to the dusty road.

The church clock creaked and chimed one.

Dogs barked at me but no one lit a candle or looked to see who was passing their door. At the edge of the town I turned off the road and on to the trails that led over the moor to Butterburn.

The heather was tough and tangled but I followed the twisting sheep trails up into the hills. If I stepped on an adder I'd have died.

But if I didn't go on then poor Old Nan would die.

After half an hour I saw her tiny cottage of tumbled stone with a roof of heather.

Everything was silent. I didn't want to disturb her. I sank on to the heather, pulled the cloak over me and slept.

When the sun rose three hours later I woke with a start. A woman was looking down at me. She was probably about forty years old but the harsh life had turned her hair grey and wrinkled her skin dry like tree bark.

'Nan!' I said.

'Young Meg,' she nodded. 'Come for a cure? At this time of the morning?'

'No, I've come to warn you about Lord Scuggate,' I told her.

'I remember him when he was young. An idle and vicious lad,' she said, shaking her head. 'His father spoiled him – oldest son, you see?'

Suddenly she looked at me sharply. 'What's he up to now?'

I rose stiffly to my feet. 'It's a long story.'

'Then come inside,' she said and walked towards the cottage without looking back. 'A tale is better told when you have goat's milk and oatcakes inside you … with heather honey.'

Far away, the Bewcastle Church clock struck five. Hounds howled. I didn't have much time.

4 The lord of a burning manor

When the clock struck twelve noon that day, Queen Mary rode up to the gates of Scuggate Manor. Her captain hammered on the great front gate. A kitchen boy tugged it open a crack and looked out.

'Where is Lord Scuggate?' the angry Captain growled.

The kitchen boy wiped his nose on his sleeve.

'Snnncccct! Dunno, pal! Lord Scuggate went out hunting on the moors at sunrise. He's never usually this late, though. His dinner's getting cold. He never likes to miss his dinners!'

The poor people of Bewcastle had come from the fields and the houses to stare at the Queen and her soldiers and servants.

Children with runny noses threw mud at the polished breastplates of her guards ...

... then ran and hid behind their mothers' skirts.

The Queen turned her flat, pasty face to the Captain of her guard. 'What sort of greeting is this for a queen?'

The Captain shrugged. 'A messenger was sent to warn Lord Scuggate last night, Your Majesty.'

She looked at the barred gate and her voice rose. 'So? Where is Lord Scuggate?'

Along the road ran a man, dripping water. He raised clouds of dust from his boots and stumbled when the sole of one flapped and let in stones. His breeches were torn and tangled with brambles. His cap slipped down over his sweating red face and his jerkin was muddy.

'I am Lord Scuggate, Your Majesty; sorry, Your Majesty, I was delayed.'

The Queen looked at him with disgust. 'Delayed?'

'I was trying to catch a witch, Your Majesty,' he whined and mopped his face with a muddy sleeve – just wiping streaks of brown on his purple cheeks.

'Where is this witch?' the Queen demanded. She wrinkled her nose as if he stank like a tramp – which he did.

'She escaped, Your Majesty. I was planning to burn her in the market place, as a sort of welcome for Your Majesty! We people of Bewcastle know how much you enjoy a good burning!' he said, flapping his hands weakly.

The Captain of the Guard
drew his sword and
rode towards Lord
Scuggate.

He smacked the Lord on the back with
the flat of the sword. 'How dare you!' he
hissed.

'Her Majesty's judges may send some
evil men to be burned. But Her Majesty
does not like to do it.'

The Captain slapped Lord Scuggate on the backside and the fat lord howled.

'Ouch! Sorry! We had heard about Bloody Mary and ...'

Smack!
'Never call her that! How dare you!'

Smack!
'Ouch! Sorry, Queen Bloody ...'

Smack!
'Ouch! Sorry ...'

The Queen turned in her saddle and looked at Scuggate Manor.

'Is this pitiful pile yours?' she asked.

'Yes, Your Queen-ness,' Lord Scuggate babbled and burbled.

'I will show you who enjoys a good burning!' She turned to her Captain. 'Burn down his house!'

Before the clock struck quarter past, the stables had been emptied of horses and the hay set alight. The servants fled as the fire spread. The powder in the gun-room exploded and the sky was filled with crimson flames and black smoke.

Queen Mary nodded. She turned her horse and led her followers away from Bewcastle. A sobbing Lord Scuggate was led away to the stocks to be pelted with rotting fruit.

There is a hill that looks down on the town. A grey-haired woman in a black dress stood on the top and shook her head.
Old Nan.

I went to The Cross Keys inn when
the Queen had gone and
was given a job as a
serving maid.

I was invisible, as ever, as I served ale to Sir James Marley and Father Walton later that evening. I sat at a table and listened to the tale Sir James had to tell.

'I'll never go out on those moors again,'
he groaned.

Father Walton's nose, sharp as a starling's
beak, twitched. 'Tell me about it.'

Sir James began and I, the invisible maid,
listened and smiled.

'We'd just crossed the stream at
Butterburn at dawn when we saw Nan.
She sat up on the ridge and looked towards
the sunrise.

'"Hag!" we called her. "Hag!" and "Witch!"'

'Lord Scuggate threw stones. They all missed and that just made him angrier. "The Devil's wrapped her in his hand. We'll never hit her with a stone," he said.

'Father Walton made the sign of the cross. "The Devil can do that," he breathed.

'That's when Scuggate said we'd have to hunt her down just like a fox. He said it would make good sport. We set off through the bracken and heather.

'The sun was getting higher and it was hot work but we didn't mind. Old Nan looked at us and hurried off over the hill. We followed her.'

'Father Walton nodded. "A witch can't fly her broomstick in the daylight."

'We reached the top of the hill and we could see Old Nan's cottage below us. We slipped the leashes off the dogs. The dogs leapt forward while the witch lifted up her skirts and ran.

'She reached the battered wooden door a moment before the howling hounds. They crashed against it just as Nan threw in the bolt,' Sir James said and his eyes glowed with the memory.

'We reached the dogs and pulled them away. I called, "Come out, Old Nan! We won't harm you!" And Scuggate hissed, "No we won't, but our dogs will tear you flesh from bone."

'I heard her shout back through the door, "If you don't want to harm me, leave me alone!"

'We pulled some bushes from the garden and he piled them up against the door. I took a flint from out of my pocket and he started up a fire.'

Father Walton nodded again. 'Best thing for a witch. Fire.'

'The bush was dry …'

'It hasn't rained for weeks.'

'Exactly, so the bush began to crackle and the gold flames took hold. Then the door began to smoulder – its ancient wood was as dry as the dust on the daisies in Old Nan's garden. The woman screamed as the door burned through.

'We stepped back to keep from being roasted alive. They saw the woman's figure, head down, burst out through the charcoal ruins of the door.'

'So, you set the dogs after her? They love to hunt a running animal. They tore her into fifty pieces, I'll bet,' Father Walton crooned and licked his thin lips.

'Ah, no,' Sir James groaned. 'That's when she used the witchcraft, isn't it?'

6 The flying witch

Sir James Marley gripped his beer mug tight as he told his tale.

'Old Nan was fast as any hare. She had a start on the dogs. We lost sight of her as she ran up to the hill top. The dogs seemed too fat and full of flesh to chase her hard!'

I smiled as I listened. I'd fed those dogs well the night before.

'Then Old Nan stopped on the crest
of a hill and looked back down at us. She
dropped out of sight. Then the strangest
thing happened. We heard a cry. "Leave me
alone!" a woman screamed. But the sound
didn't come from over the hill. We looked
back at the smoking ruin of Old Nan's
house. And there she stood beside the
doorway!'

'Witchcraft,' Father Walton groaned and crossed himself again. 'What did you do?'

'We lumbered back down the hill to the cottage, of course. The dogs' noses told them she was over the top of the hill. Their eyes told them she was running downhill from the house. They ran round in circles then followed us back down the hill.'

'But did they catch her?'

'I'm coming to that,' Sir James said and supped his ale. 'The woman disappeared into a small clump of trees. When we reached it she wasn't in sight. Then we heard her cry again ...

'You had her trapped in the wood,' the priest smirked.

'No! The voice came from behind us. She was at the top of the hill again! She couldn't have run! She must have flown. We set off back up the hill and she ran. It was a struggle but when we got to the top … she'd gone.

'We heard her cry, "Leave me alone!" and there she was. At the edge of the wood. 'All morning we chased her. When we thought she was in the wood she was on the hill top. When we thought she was on the hill top she was down in the wood.'

'Didn't the dogs catch her?' Father Walton asked.

'I'll swear at one time they did. I saw them race up to her on the top of the hill. There was sweat in my eyes but I'll swear they got to her. She just stretched out a hand and patted them! They wagged their miserable tails!'

The priest moaned. 'You cannot fight the Devil!'

Of course, I knew they hadn't been fighting the Devil.

I knew they had been chasing two women – Old Nan was one. I was the other. We'd made a white wig from sheep's wool for me to wear. The hunters never got close enough to see who was really on top of the hill. Nan just stayed near the wood.

We took it in turns to cry, 'Leave me alone!' and we watched the men run up and down the hill all the hot summer morning.

When the dogs caught me, of course they let me pat them! I was the maid that fed them!

'But that wasn't the worst,' Sir James said and held out his mug for more ale.

I filled it and smiled.

7 Old Nan's new guard

I knew the worst.
At last Sir James Marley
of Roughsike and
Lord Scuggate
stumbled
back to
Bewcastle
that
morning.

Nan and I came together at the smouldering ruin of her cottage.

We heard the church clock strike a quarter to twelve and we heard his Lordship yell, 'The Queen! She'll be here soon!'

'No parade! No witch-burning!' Sir James wailed.

Nan and I watched as the two men rushed to the bridge together and, in their panic, crashed into one another and fell into the river. It's lucky the river was low after the hot summer weather or they'd have drowned.

But they hit a pool where the town drain runs out. They came out spluttering, smelling strongly. They did not smell of sweet heather, either. It was then that Lord Scuggate ran to meet the Queen – dripping and smelling of the town toilets.

The friendly men in the local tavern laughed when I told them the story of the trick we'd played on the foul Lord Scuggate.

Next day, they climbed the hill and built a new cottage for Nan, fine enough to keep out the wicked winds that whipped Butterburn each winter.

No one helped Lord Scuggate to rebuild the manor. And he had lost all he owned in the fire. He moved in with his friend, Sir James at Roughsike. They deserve each other.

He won't be back to bother Old Nan again. And, even if he did, he'd find she has two fierce dogs to guard her. Lord Scuggate's dogs!

How did she tame the beasts? With kindness? Or with witchcraft?

Only Old Nan knows!

Afterword: Old Nan's story

The Maid, the Witch and the Cruel Queen is a story based on real people and events in Tudor times.

Mary Tudor became queen when her father, Henry VIII, died in 1553. She was a Catholic and wanted everyone in England to worship at Catholic churches. She made a new law that said people who refused could be burned. From 1555 till she died in 1558, three hundred men and women were burned.

The people of England learned to hate her and to call her 'Bloody Mary'. They had bonfires and parties when she died. Mary's sister, Elizabeth I, took the throne and stopped the burning of people who refused to worship in Catholic churches.

But killing 'witches' still went on.

In Tudor Britain, it was against the law to practise witchcraft. In England, the punishment was to be hanged, while in Scotland, witches were burned.

Most of the people accused of being witches were harmless old women who had no one to protect them. From 1450 to 1598 over thirty thousand people in Europe were executed as witches.

But there are some stories of women accused of witchcraft who got away with it. One of these stories was about a woman in northern England known as 'Old Nan'.

It was said that the local men

tried to hunt her down, but when they chased her to the top of a hill she appeared at the bottom. No matter where they chased her she seemed to appear somewhere else calling, 'Leave me alone!'

Did Old Nan use witchcraft? Or did she use a trick like the one in this story? Was there ever such a person as Old Nan? Or is she just a legend?

Only Old Nan knows!

The Actor, the Rebel and the Wrinkled Queen

Elizabeth I is a mean queen –
with hands like claws, a wrinkled
white face and rotting teeth.
James Foxton is a young player
in Shakespeare's theatre company.
When the actors are caught
up in a rebellion, James finds himself
at the cold Queen's mercy ...

The Thief, the Fool and the Big Fat King

In the reign of King Henry VIII, London is full of cheats and villains. When James and his parents try to get the better of Henry, they find he wants to play games of his own. Can they challenge the all-powerful King – and win?

The Prince, the Cook and the Cunning King

When a thin, pale boy called
Lambert claims he's the rightful
heir to the throne, King Henry VII
is furious! Mean King Henry has
clever ways of dealing with this
young impostor. Can Eleanor,
the maid, discover the truth –
and what will it mean for Lambert?